Review of ⅃
by David Willson, Book Reviewer
The Vietnam Veterans of America

"I read Roy Eisenstein's novella, *Blacktop, No Map,* in one sitting. The author served with the 1st Signal Brigade in 1968-69; his main character is a Vietnam veteran who has PTSD. The writing in this breathless amalgam of a road novella and film noire script is fun to read. I'll bet it was fun to write, too.

The novella is sprinkled with references to the Vietnam War. They all passed muster. Some that stood out: 'I woke up from another night in the rice paddies,' 'the damp rice paddies of my soul.' Also: 'a guy named Hank who has a VC scar and a platoon of dead brothers.'

No false notes in this book tarnished the relentless forward thrust of the narrative, and I enjoyed it mightily. I highly recommend this story to those who want to enjoy an afternoon in the sunshine with a cold drink, reading something to take their mind off their troubles and propel them into a world with a tough but sensitive hero and a beautiful younger woman who adores him and asks no questions about where they are bound and why.

I've been there; I totally get the appeal of such a story."

BLACKTOP, NO MAP

By Roy Eisenstein

EyeZenMedia.Weebly.com

Special thanks to

Freddy Tran Nager

Dale Griffiths Stamos

Jeanne Ardito

Theresa Lee

I wasn't always dead. No, I wasn't always a distant, cold satellite so removed from the sun. I had fire and madness and the wild dog passions of a dreamer, but that was before reality put its stamp of disapproval on me. Before choppers broke the silence of adolescent optimism and patriotism and the word "sorties" became part of my vocabulary.

Last night I dreamt of that old alphabet soup of hot LZs with the zing of AKs dropping GIs under the gusts of Huey rotors. I could smell the distinctive metallic bite of gunpowder in the noise of commands yelled through the chopped wind and howls of wounded and dying comrades. I felt the sweat and heat in a world gone mad while trying to keep my mind together looking for cover. Heart tattooing inside my ribcage, pulse racing through me, and the ever present "what the fuck" in a universe falling apart. Until I woke up to that old question, where the hell am I? Where am I?

These old scenes started to return two weeks ago when my mailbox kicked me in the gut with the arrival of my ex-wife's wedding invitation, with its silver, embossed Apple Chancery font so delicately announcing her upcoming nuptials. Not that I want to dance that song anymore, but Jesus Christ, how'd she work all this out while I'm still digging my way out of the debris of our divorce?

It's been ten years and I've been in and out of a number of shallow lakes of love since, but I never really knew how I felt because there was too much numb to get through.

But now I look to the form sleeping next to me and a flood of contradictions assail me to the point of emotional vertigo. She almost smiles in her snugged snooze unaware of the mission I awoke from, and without an inkling of what the US Postal system has done to me.

She's a bit younger than I am, so I have no idea if she can even imagine the noise in my skull. How could she, even though we've been sharing each other for almost two years now. Just too much unsaid, I guess.

My ex. Man, she was there when I got back to "the World." Went through all the changes with me. Held on when I was losing my foothold. Gave me some solid ground when I no longer trusted the Earth. When my country no longer felt like a welcome home, but a dark swirl of criticism and anger.

One day we turned to face one another and realized that somehow a lot of acreage had sprawled between us and we lost our grip on one another and she wanted to move on. But those were yesterdays.

The rest of the night passes in a parade of minutes all crowded with questions and memories. I keep looking around and this Los Angeles cottage is suddenly alien. Nothing looks familiar, most of all myself. How'd I get here? Wasn't the sun and surf supposed to redeem me? There's movement inside me that demands my attention, a need to change the air I breathe, a longing for not being where I am. I feel that old rustling that begs for motion.

I have to leave LA. I am disintegrating here to the point where I won't even leave a chalk outline on the pavement, when even the mirror becomes just another wall and no matter how loud I cry out I create no echo.

I can almost hear the siren of the east coast whispering something in that old seductive call. Some shadowed promise of finding my skin again back there, that I've gotten lost out here in this paradise. I'm not a surfer. I'm not a suntan or a "dude." I'm concrete and asphalt. I'm hard angles and direct statements. At least I think I am, and so I can't fake "laid back" when my soul is the D Train, or the Belt Parkway.

Unusually cold end of summer night and I hear the howl of loneliness in the air as some things unfinished stalk every thought. Old ghosts in whispers that won't get lost in the wind, hints of what I've carried too long, who I was and don't want to be.

Just one of those nights that want to tell you something about yourself that you've been burying too long. You can't bury something that isn't dead. It always claws its way back up to the surface.

She wakes up too and looks up at me in that way that says, "Whatever you're thinking about, include me." That atmosphere in her eyes that surrounds me and is my oxygen. Who is this creature?

She fills the space around us with soft things that come out of her so naturally and with such ease that although I crave to cover my tired life with them they also make me see all the rough edges and sharp quills that bristle from me, all the wounds and scars that leave a trail of anger and distrust wound so tightly that they could snap like traps.

She could put a clipping from some plant in a tin can, place it on a windowsill somewhere unimportant and transform my cynical darkness into something tender.

But tonight something has to break loose. Something has to set fire to these bridges and flee the torment of feeling meaningless. I have to tear free from this choking stagnation that's rising all around me. But how do I tell her? She seems so at home here.

She listens to my vague plans and without a flinch or a hint of doubt she suitcases a few things, we lock the door, get in the car and take the night road towards forever in a mood that makes the sky come in close. What the hell, neither of us have jobs that mean anything. No one will really miss us. And god knows we won't miss them.

We are in motion and now anything can happen. Movement attracts energy. Invites possibilities. Challenges the world to come in and stir the sediments of dreams from the bottom and bring them up to the surface where chance can get a taste of them.

The top is down so we let our hair go wild in the cold night like snakes on fire while the music on the radio makes dangerous promises. There's just something so damn American about the gas pedal and the open road.

Los Angeles is a desert by the sea, and the nights have a chill. Grabbing the 10 we push away from the sea and through the sprawl of urban suburbs, but eventually we bust free of the LA Basin and into the rest of the world.

We're heading east through a landscape that floats in silence under a sniper's moon and makes the eyes believe in things the mind knows don't exist, or doesn't want to believe are possible.

The heater warms our feet and legs while our faces sting crimson in the night air. We drive for hours until the coolness disappears with the first touches of the rising sun and the darkness flees westward towards all we'd left behind.

Where the hell are we going? Sure, I've got New York in the crosshairs, but what then? I don't know any more than changing our geography, but I think when I get there I'll relocate my finger prints. Yeah, that's where I'll make sense of all this.

Morning comes up hot and angry and quickly presses down on everything with a searing vengeance that grows more hostile with the approach of noon. This is most of the interior of California, an endless, bone dry forever. An arid sprawl of commanding emptiness.

Stopping to refuel is a taste of hell, so the rag-top goes up to hide us from the broiler and save our flesh.

The Mojave runs flat and long and desolate as the Interstate cuts a laser-beam line due east, and off in every distance gray, naked mountains float lonely on some shimmering vapor flame that makes me think I'm dreaming.

My mind fills with images of the settlers coming west through these lands in their Conestoga wagons with children, and horses, and a dog or two. Pots and pans clanging in complaint against every stone or rut the wooden wheels suffered. All their lives packed in, tied onto or dragging behind.

What drove them? What fire of faith in them pushed them deeper into this dry death? What made them believe it would ever end?

Our tank is full, the windshield washed and the highway passing under us, and although we feel the rage of speed and the snarl of the engine it feels like hours pass without ever really getting anywhere.

We've taken a big bite out of the western edge of Arizona when the oil runs out and the engine seizes. We are going nowhere. She tries to call her daddy from a gas station payphone for some help, but he is on another line selling linoleum and wallpaper to people who are just trying to cover things.

Her father is a man who wears a cheap toupee from Hong Kong like a drunken waiter in a greasy restaurant, and reeks of a cologne outlawed by the Geneva Convention.

He speaks through a practiced handshake and a rehearsed sincerity while he guesses the strength of your wallet by assessing the condition of your shoes.

The sort of man who could pick your pocket with a smile.

He hates me for the way his daughter looks at me and so he tells everyone lies about me. That I was the bastard boy of a whore and a shoe salesman from Lido just to hide the tracks of his own mobile home lineage.

There was no way he'll put out a hand unless his palm is facing up. So there's no use in asking him to throw us a life preserver, and so without his help we just walk until the sun's determination is greater than ours, and we surrender to the fact that we need a new ride.

We pull out all our folded greens and get a used car from some corner-lot-Satan with a bad tooth job and a bowtie while the little red white and blue triangular plastic flags snap in the dirty breeze implying that any purchase here would be an act of patriotism.

He swears to the reliability of the car and the low price was because he had to move stock or lose it. I don't believe him, but the thin posture of my cash flow doesn't leave me many options.

The damn thing takes us as far as the edge of New Mexico before it too bleeds to death and once again we have no wheels of our own.

Sometimes life seems to enjoy messing with us. Some cosmic sadism that implies the possible existence of a cruel and bored deity.

My ex and I passed through this state a million years ago on our way to California. We had dreams of a new life out west where your car battery never refuses to start because it's been snowing all night. I was still haunted back then, but I believed in her optimism and the curative powers of love. And now she's loving someone else enough to remarry. Okay, it's not that I'm not happy for her, it's that I'm just miserable for me. So she can have LA. It's hers now. Besides, I know my soul is back in New York. I mean, isn't it?

Two states and two cars. At this rate we'd own a fleet of dead wheels before we hit the heartland.

I kick and beat and curse the old piece of crap as if it were doing this to me out of some act of spite. Her laughter breaks around me as I throw my little fit. She has a way of believing everything will always work out somehow. Some part of her doesn't see the dirty handiwork of some malevolent misfortune. Instead, even through the tender bruises of her unfinished childhood, all she sees is the revelation of the comic underbelly of it all. She laughs into tears as I wrestle and box the indifferent heap that refuses to rise from death and continue to bear us on our journey until my anger joins her humor and I too see the foolishness of the battle I am waging.

She wants to marry me, but I think I'll get tired of her little tattoo in time and so I dance around the question that is always just hanging there in the unspoken air between us.

There was a time when someone with a wound like hers would blind me to the altar in the drunken stumble of lust, but I'm angrier nowadays and so I don't step into that hole like I used to.

My divorce left a crater in my trust so deep that I can love without loving. I can see it, smell it, feel and yet live it as a mere observer. I was robbed of something and didn't realize that I was the thief. And here I am, this wraith trying to pass as a human being. Making the noises of a pumping heart where only a scar remains. Going through the motions like some dark pantomime. A mockery of all things tender. A dead soldier whose name didn't make it on the wall.

Luckily a junker takes the beast off our hands and gives us some presidents in exchange. We're not flush, but it helps. We watch as he drives off with our car in tow like someone dragging away a dead animal.

We leave the desert by train and keep heading east where our Southern California clothing won't protect us, and the dull glaze of our eyes will make us look like bait in an old Chinese-food take-out carton, ready for the hook.

She holds my arm as I drown in my seat and the countryside moves by outside the window like a slide show. And the moon looks on indifferently as poets write diabetic verse to it while gazing up at that silver disk. They scratch out their romantic lines of the illusion of a relationship caressed by love when all they really want is to get laid.

Am I sounding too cynical?

She sleeps seamlessly in the even pattern of steel wheels on tracks laid across wooden ties. The heartbeat of jolts in sync with her easy breaths. She knows where she is on earth and I am a man without a map.

One thing about movement, you're constantly somewhere you're not.

Finally Albuquerque sprawls flat and faceless around the green scar of the Rio Grande while the Sandia Mountains stand silent witness to the thirsty grid of houses and apartments and shopping malls that never stop being built.

Even the dry places on earth are filling up with humanity. Seems our race of beings abhor unused space. We actually take great pride in removing all traces of original design. Like gift-wrapping something beautiful because we don't trust that gift by itself is enough.

We pick up another ride near Santa Fe for a few hundred bucks.
Nothing to look at, just fenders, bumpers and torn seats wrapped around an old V-8 that leaves dark oily suicide notes everywhere it parks. It has California plates and an air freshener hanging from the rearview that only hinted at better times. California plates, eh? Some synchronistic continuity in the universe? An omen right out of the bowels of Detroit? A mystical talisman with four on the floor? Or just another random bit of coincidental bullshit.

Soon we are on the leeward side of I-40 at 75mph, leaving the high chaparral and by early morning we are pounding through Texas forever.

Dry dirt and charred grasslands spread out like the ugly girl at the prom just waiting for someone to take her. Anyone.

Another small motel gives us a bed at a cheap rate, but I wake up from another night in the rice paddies, so I'm not very chipper. In my mind this is not Mr. Rogers' neighborhood. No, I served a year in Texas when I returned stateside, so this place has a few thorns in my dark side, and so she and I are having a small war of our own over nothing she'd done. But I still tear into her. I storm out all my venom like a mad fool with no one to blame.

She looks at me while I rage around this little room gathering up our belongings, then quietly helps as I throw our things back in the car.

My hands on the wheel I breathe my unspoken fire in the silence. I just unloaded on her for no goddamn reason and now we are just sitting there in that hot little car while I think of a million ways to tell her to run for her life. To go back to LA. To escape from my madness while she can, and her hand suddenly finds the back of my neck and strokes me gently. A soft hand that merely plays with the hair on the back of my head, and I feel a million crows fly out of me. All my knives fall to the ground and if I had the courage to I'd cry all over her. I'd throw myself into her arms and let it all go.

I start the engine without saying a word and we drive.

In the burn of daylight we tear a slice out of the panhandle on a diagonal run that smashes us into the eastern corner of Oklahoma and onward as the last days of heat fuse our asses to the vinyl seats under a glare so intense we even squint at night.

My mind hovers somewhere in the dry landscape that dominates everything while part of me feels the damp rice paddies of my soul.

We stop here and there for food or gas or to stretch the bolts of our joints and remind ourselves of our ability to stand upright. But even walking about on the side of the road you can still feel the vibration of the pistons reverberating through your marrow.

I guess this is how a sailor feels when he first hits shore after a long time at sea.

The only news I get to read along the way is the scrawl carved into the paint in gas station restrooms. With crushed smokes on the urine soaked tiles, scarred mirrors and no hand towels.

She sleeps for miles with her head against the window. It doesn't matter to her where she is, she feels tired and she sleeps. Me? Hell, before I can drop into that peaceful abyss I have to wear myself out so that my mind simply crashes in exhaustion. And even then my thoughts keep me going. What's that old expression about the sleep of the innocent? I guess that says something about me, eh?

I listen to the static radio that hints at reception now and then. I inhale the mixture of coolant and gasoline, and the dust that's been blowing around these parts since the 1920s.

I can smell her hair and sweet flesh in the mixture of cowboy wind and my own longing.

I throw doubting glances at her long legs and up across her calm features, and I don't know who the hell she is. I wonder where her dreams take her, and why such a creature would want to attach herself to a ghost like me.

A shower and some clean sheets alone sure seem like heaven right about now. Even just a few hours by myself to figure out who I am and where I'm headed holds promises of a çure.

We pull off in the middle of nowhere important to get something in our bellies.

The diner has the usual trade, belt buckles, Stetsons, boots and bellies, tobacco stained teeth and moustaches.

There are no Japanese cars in this parking lot.

Naugahyde vinyl seats and Formica table tops. A counter with a row of spinning stools, small juke-boxes at each booth, fluorescent lights, and an endless smell of bacon and toast. I'm ready.

A pear-shaped middle-aged woman pours nonstop greasy coffee into thick ceramic cups, and even with her white underarms flapping and her too-much eye shadow she is a goddess to these canyon faced rustics who study her every move.

Their crude sexual insinuations evoke schoolgirl laughter and a free glazed cruller here and there as she adds a sway to her step and uses her eyes and smile like someone she never was.

She breaks away from them with a cute remark causing an eruption of male laughter that leaves a smile deep on her face as she comes by and takes our order amidst a shower of "darlin's," and "honey's," like she's known us all along and we are here for the usual.

Our food comes and we eat our eggs and hash browns like strangers sharing the check. I don't feel like conversation and I can't even look up across the table at her because I fear the invitations she'd read into my glances and I want to be alone in my head just for a while. So my eyes follow the toast as I mop the yellow yolk, and still she chirps about the trip and her foot touches mine under the table and I like it and don't like it and I like it.

Night catches us off guard so we fall into a matchbox motel built in the 50s for a nation of Chevrolets looking for America. A time when they gave you dishes whenever you filled the tank. When someone would run out and check your air and oil and clean your windshield while asking you how you're doing and "Where ya headed?"

The room is as tight as an old suit but clean under the bare bulb stuck in the toothpaste stucco ceiling. It's a place to stop.

No air-conditioning, no heat, a color TV that carries both local stations, and enough fresh towels to spoil me.

We knock off a fifth of inexpensive mash and then wrestle that double bed for hours. A pounding exchange of grunts and groans and she wins the best two out of three, but I hold onto the championship, for now.

Morning arrives with sarcastic cruelty and the cheap whiskey we had shared last night rattles around in my dome like loose stones in a metal cup, and I wish I had been less selfish and let her drink more of it so I'd have drunken less. But too late for that.

Needing medicine we find a little joint along the way. We elbow the bar and order the cure from a guy named Hank who has a VC scar and a platoon of dead brothers he wears on his face while he tries to laugh through his cigarette cough. I keep my secrets to myself. I know if I open that hatch it could start a stampede I won't be able to stop. A part of me wants to grab him and hold him as a brother. Welcome him home. Lock in that embrace of those who know. But I'm frozen and restrained by binding chains around my soul that won't let me.

From his side of the bar the patrons line up on their stools, a shooting gallery that he nails one shot at a time.

She looks soft in the reflected neon light of the beer signs while Hank opens old wounds about a daughter who ran off with a radio weatherman who chased a gig up to Urbana, Illinois.

She listens to him with every part of her existence. She has a way of taking what you've got without leaving you empty. Helping you carry your parcels of grief without the insult of sympathy. She can make a stranger feel like he's found his way home.

My eyes trace her profile like a blind man caressing a tender story in Braille, and somewhere between the liquor and her unprotected innocence I feel the warm glue of passion rise in me. That same old hunger that always had the maps to my defenses and could slip in under my radar and slam me into a submission hold that tears "I love you" out of me with fatal results.

But the dance has already begun because some unseen hand plays all the right chords and dizzy in this dervish I take her arm and in the public of a state park, hidden in a copse of trees I ride her hard and long and make promises with my body while a river of romance flows from my mouth to her ear.

I mean every word of it and it scares the hell out of me.

Soon we are back on the Interstate, her head in my lap, she naps. Loving me like a newfound religion. And the accelerator can not help me outrun those old doubts that rise up behind me. A rugged landscape of losses.

When a marriage fails it's a personal thing. You're never really prepared for it. You never enter such a union thinking you won't make the distance. That this thing is doomed from the get go. And when that dream, that romantic fairytale of promises falls apart you're left with a broken world. A place where things don't align. The basis of your system of beliefs in how the universe operates no longer applies to anything and so you're suddenly groping around for a new template. You're struggling to find some chart to give you a sense of how the game is supposed to be played since the old diagrams no longer make sense.

She was a good woman. And I thought I was a good man. We had love and laughs and it all rumbled along and seemed solid enough so when she left I was caught by the sucker punch of it.

Never saw it coming, no warnings, no premonitions, not a hint, a clue or the slightest foreshadowing of her discontent. Just a surgical slice and my line was cut and I was floating away into a dense fog of accusatory questions to myself about how I screwed up.

I remember walking past a shop and seeing something in a window and wondering if she'd like it too, and then realizing she was no longer in the equation. That habit of thinking in two was now torn quite violently into a one. Didn't matter if she'd like the item or not, she was gone from the story.

I was with her a long time and I forgot how to be just me. I bumped into some really bad relationships after that. The first one was a sexual animal who always needed her fix and I have to admit there were times I was not the man for the job. I was broken and needing something else but was so lost I even blamed myself for that.

And there were others and they went better, but I always seemed to be sitting outside the campfire looking in. I could feel the passion, the animal needs fed, but I couldn't feel the heat.

And all along I should have realized that I'd never really come home from the tropics. That all I could ever offer any woman was this fragment of me while my insides were still walking point somewhere she could never even imagine. Why would any woman want that?

So here I am again. hanging on the blacktop at 75 mph in a rush somewhere eastward under a low hot sky while carrion crows pick the center lane clean right up to the last minute and then scatter to the sky until we are gone again and then return to finish the feast. And next to me, looking out at the fleeing landscape is this soft heart who loves me.

My thoughts grease through sloppy memories and half-truths that shame me and blame me and drag me down to where I am, heading nowhere and getting there fast. Bouncing back and forth through time and relationships in some bumper-pool hell and I seem to know nothing.

She sits up into the dry wind that is outside and inside the car, that throws her hair in crazy patterns, and she drinks some bottled water and tosses me a smile that asks way too much of me while at the same time somehow tending to my wounds. Who is this being and how does she do that?

The sun finally disappears somewhere behind us, and the ink blue night is waiting straight ahead.

Pinpricks of light break through and the moon hangs there, just a circle of ice, while the highway still moans from the heat and the kamikaze insects explode on the windshield in Jackson Pollack-Rorschach sacrifices.

Our escape is a slaughter we ignore as the wiper blades spread the carnage in waxy green, red, and yellow swipes that will not wash away. So under the invasive surgery lights of a gas station I squeegee the windshield of the massacre. Collateral damage.

The attendant in the glass box watches me with dead eyes. Listening to the local radio religion which makes him promises of eternal resurrection in exchange for a small donation.

He wants to come back to life for more of this? To live again? He wants this to go on and on? A life of hoping some passing license plate will stop and buy some soft drinks or beef jerky, pick up batteries or a local magnet for their refrigerator? I'll take death. The long sleep. The silent unknown. God knows I can use the rest.

The little numbers on the pump ascend at a manic pace as the sweet poison smell of 87 octane runs into the vein, down into the steel belly, feeding the metal heart, through the soul, under the spirit, and coming all the way from the House of Saud.

She wants to drive so I slump in the shotgun seat, roll down the window, and let the night wash me away.

I think I slept or imagined I slept or hallucinated or prayed or dreamt of sleep, or astral projected, but I'm awake now and time goes by in clips or chunks or spasms of images of places I've been to, or wanted to be, or may not even exist, while the night fragments into this mosaic of alternating desperation and hope and fear and desire and I wish I were driving so I could make believe I was doing something, because it all seems so meaningless and in every scenario I reflect upon I'm the common denominator. Me. Starring in every scene.

I finally doze for real and sink back into a time and place when my heart pounded. When in my foolish youth I helped B-52s leave the ground, fill the sky and then go off to do their dirty work. They'd climb so high above the reach of anti-aircraft batteries, up in   heaven where surface to air missiles could not touch their silver bodies, so deep in God's lap they'd cruise until they'd unload their bellies in a blind seeding of death so very far below. And the world beneath erupted into flames and horror. Too far away to hear. Too remote to feel. Too abstract to absorb its meaning.

In that sleep I see the faces of those I'd never seen. The old, the young, the poor. The fields of rice, the jungles, the villages and cities, the harbors and train yards, the homes and factories, schools and hospitals, military and non-military, the bombs did not care.

And I am torn from there. Ripped back to the present and this highway and the hum of the motor, the rumble of the road, and her innocent profile is illuminated by the wash of passing headlights, as she keeps her eyes on the traffic ahead.

There's an uneasiness to being alone with myself, my thoughts, my life, when I know I've been faking it. When every surface is a mirror confronting me and mocking me. When each little lie is gaining on me and all the practiced deceptions of confidence are crushed beneath the boots of failure or regret.

A haunting echo of every line of bullshit I ever uttered. Hard copy evidence of each little egotistical foray into self-promotion and false resume` just to impress some skirt, or status the boys, or get some position I knew I'd be

ejected from once they found out how much I didn't know
or care.

No wonder I'm exhausted.

To save some money we pull into a rest area, roll up
the windows almost to the top, lock the doors and fall into
that almost coma we both need or want or feel we owe our
bodies, only this time with her snugged up into my clutch
of arms I go into a quieter darkness where my demons let
me rest.

Daylight finally returns and heats our tin can. I
wake up with my body folded around the steering wheel,
ripe with that four-door airtight stench and creak. She
sprawls the back seat, a kitten on an old coat. I guess at
some point she woke up and relocated for the sake of space.

I want to peel my clothes off and burn them.

Clothing, the old skin of cloth that stamps any
photograph with the decade of that hour. A once cool
haircut that now looks silly. A footnote of insignificant
details that define us without saying who we really are, just
some dictate of fashion or common garb for the times that
somehow implies and lies that we were more advanced or
more together than the humans that struggled on this planet
before us in their silly hats and such.

Photographs. Photo albums. What are they? In any
home they lay about like a dishonest history book. All
smiles and arms around shoulders. Good times registered
page after asinine page. Oh each family so happy from
birthday to birthday. The Christmas joy, the trip to the
amusement park. The endless stream of grinning ecstasy
that conceals the heartbreaks, denies the quarrels and
abuses, the disappointment. Loving kissing photos that
show no hint of the infidelities. And then those heroic
pictures of soldier sons and proud parents. The welcome
home cakes and girlfriends clinging to those returning
arms. And no one sees the broken promises in his eyes, the

cracked and trampled trust in his heart. No one sees the dead who now and always will be with him.

I want to stand under running water and watch the soap-suds swirl through my toes and down through the drain to some unseen world where all our dirt mingles in some sea of what we were. I want to stand there until every vestige of my pain is washed from my flesh and my thoughts and my dreams. To be scrubbed clean and fresh so I can start again. So I can be someone better. So I can leave this load of darkness behind me.

Just then she rises with an imprint of her sleeve deep in her cheek. Some broken promise of youth stolen in the lie of one night. The first signs of time when the flesh slows to recover. But hell, she's got plenty of time.

She looks at me as if I have some answers, as if I know something of the world, of tomorrow. She trusts some part of me that doesn't exist, some deception in my walk, or my glance, some illusion I perfected to scarecrow my greatest fears. Or just some piece of me I cannot find.

I feel the weight of my ignorance lean on me. The tonnage of questions I could never answer, the truth of my weakness howling in the painful silence of my flesh as she presses her body against mine for safety and I can never save her, save her from me, from my doubts, from my long silences, from the way I can look at her and not see her at all because if I do I might catch a glimpse of myself. If I really see her I might have to surrender this curse and live up to who I can be.

Who could I be? I used to draw and paint as a kid. I might've grown to be an artist. Evolved into someone whose brush strokes moved people. Added to life some charge of emotion that resonated as something constructive, not a man still unsure of who he is. Not a ghost who never came to rest.

And then she looks up directly into my eyes and smiles. And that, for a moment tears away the thorns and hackles from my soul. That smile that she has which burns down walls and slams so deeply into my core. And then for an instant, for a brief slice of time I'm weightless and I don't want to be anywhere else on Earth.

We kiss and she touches my hair and my face with her knowing hands and all the bleeding stops.

Later once again the miles run under the car as we write our story on the broken white line and she sings along with the radio. She doesn't even know the song so she's faking it. I want to laugh but I don't want to break the spell. She makes up words and they fit. They seal the cracks and seams in the universe where pieces are missing.

Driving, driving, driving. And she falls into a book and disappears among the pages for a while so that I'm left with the road to myself.

I hold the wheel with both hands out of some belief that I'll disappear if I let go. That I'll drift off into forever, breaking up like smoke in a storm.

The sound of my blood-pump assures me that I'm still there, that it isn't just the darkness of forever that's wrapped around this flickering light.

And rising from her reading she starts laughing. I ask her what is so funny and she loses all control and snorts and giggles insanely with tears running down her face. The more I ask the more she laughs and soon I'm laughing too without any idea why. She gasps for air, I sputter out my last laughs and there is a calm in the air which makes me forget myself long enough for a smile to take up some real estate on my face.

Oklahoma is flat and dry. Short-grass prairie and high plains where the winds blew the farms away in a chalky dry vengeance leaving only natural gas, crushed stone, Portland cement, sand, gravel, gypsum, and iodine to be scraped, dug or sifted from this bitter surface. No more crops to be raised and reaped here.

Oil wells and pumps sit on the flesh of the land, steel mosquitoes sucking black blood from beneath the surface while diners and car lots and fast food chains line up in cloned towns where anyone with a dream or drive would flee at the first glimmer of opportunity to some other place. To any other place where something happens. Where life's high point weren't the senior prom followed by routine jobs, automatic marriage, popping out babies, and taking out oppressive loans for a shoebox home with a driveway, a pickup, and a shot at the mundane.

I'm dying little deaths just passing through this lie of civilization.

The only reason a stranger would stop in these places would be to fill the tank, get directions, or live in the Witness Protection Program.

So we blow through to the Ouachita Mountains that lifts us up to where trees grow with pride and rivers are born and then run down into the parched lowlands. But up in the mountains we clear the dirt from our mouths and eyes and drive though places where the sky rests upon the Earth.

A sweeter air passes through the car and our lungs with a new sense of hope, escape, and possibilities, as we push higher and higher.

The mountains run across the eastern part of the state and half way through Arkansas, but we climb northeast towards Missouri.

The old horses pound under the hood and with every other fill up we dump more oil down the black thirsty grease hole in respect to the hemorrhage.

Funny, but she never asks me where we're going. Never questions about our destination. She doesn't seem to care. She's perfectly content everywhere, anywhere. How does she do that? She's excited by the process, not the results. She's present. She's right here right now in the moment while I'm always gazing over the horizon in some

20

anxious expectation. New York, Canada, Mexico, doesn't matter to her as long as we are together. She has the ability to sit still while I'm the one whose foot is tapping, whose fingers are drumming.

We finally stop in a small roadside market from some other decade where we pick up the "fixin's" for sandwiches, some beers and a crossword puzzle book that she scratches at for wordless miles and takes us 3 down and 19 across right over the state line.

Each cycle of the engine puts the west coast further behind us, and memories seem to evaporate out of the tailpipe, like a sweater unraveling, caught on some distant hook or snare until finally you're naked and undefined and you get to start over, recreate yourself, chapter one all over again.

Not sure what I'm running from or to, but I have to get away, or to it in a hurry. Maybe the old neighborhood will restore my reflection. Maybe the schoolyards or handball courts will bring back my shadow. Something has to click or I'll continue to disintegrate and blow away with the wind.

But at last the movement of a car on an open road makes me feel a sense of purpose. Mission. That there is some destination worth getting to. And the challenge of making good time as if some critical deadline has to be met in the spirit of the Pony Express. I hate the fatal rust of inertia.

Life passes when you're sitting still, punching the clock, staring at the wall, waiting for someone else or some timer to set you loose, but when you move, step into the swirl, throw yourself into the river of things, that's when everything speeds up, and all the atoms of your life start to smash into chance and danger, potential and luck. Things begin to happen and change and each moment has its own importance and you breathe with fire and all the doors and windows bust open and anything can find its way in, and all the dragons can get out. So here we are, two clown spirits raging in a northeast slant across a continent nation with only this vague destination in mind. No ultimate goal line to cross and score, only a city that makes no promises. A target from the past onto which I've projected so much hope. But for now it's just the road itself, and us, wild and free and unstoppable. No force in the universe can halt our charge .

Then suddenly a tire blows in Missouri on the 60 just outside of Aurora, north of Monett.

The rolling landscape is being devoured and the front left explodes as if something rammed us. Bang! So I take my foot off the gas and wrestle to maintain control, like saving a drowning man who in a panic, is flailing and pulling me down. While that banging rhythm of rubber reminds me of Huey Cobras coming in to evac us from a fire fight in the bush where life was so goddamn cheap.

Large hunks of smoking rubber tear away under us until they're launched out the back while ripping down to the rim.

The sound of raw metal against the hardtop, the flash of welding sparks, the smell of steel grinding is going on forever until the awkward limp onto the shoulder ends in dust and smoke and I have difficulty peeling my hands free from the wheel as an 18 wheeler rages by us in an unsympathetic storm of speed and size.

A profound silence sits on us as all the possibilities play out in our heads. All the gory details of the "what ifs" and the "we almosts" run wordless between us.

We sit there, hearts machine gunning until we fall into each other's arms and kiss like a long awaited reunion. Each heavy breath a celebration, each noise of passion, an anthem.

Right there on the highway's edge we make love like two wolverines in a blender. Tearing one another apart in the savage ecstasy of being alive.

Afterwards she waits in the sunshine and watches as I play the man and pull the aging spare from the trunk, jack up the front end and set things right. I can feel her eyes on the sinews of my arms as I spin the lugs free and the sweat bleeds through my t-shirt. She always said she liked my smell. That I had a real clean, male scent about me. Hearing that can make a man feel like man.

And then finally we are moving again.

Funny thing about hustling the highway, after a few days of roading, being in one place too long feels like something is missing and I start to ache for the hum and pulse of pistons vibrating through my every cell in sync with my heartbeat. A I itch to get going again, this need for motion, never feeling that I ever arrive because all destinations feel like a stopover since I don't really know what the hell I am looking for anyway.

But once the pace is set, the roll is locked into motion, the routine of it settles down and conversations rest, the mind starts to poke around your insides looking for something. Like your tongue trying to find some small artifact of a meal to wrangle out of some wedge of teeth.

My mind seems to be an excellent archeologist of grief. It always finds some forgotten relic of discomfort to examine and scrutinize to the point of agony.

Like, why don't I fit inside my own skin? Ever since I got back to the States nowhere is home. Why don't I belong here or there or anywhere? Why do I always want to be somewhere I'm not and not be anywhere I am. Why?

My foot presses harder on the pedal to get me out of the present and somewhere down the road to the maybe of the unknown. Away from the flame that's consuming me incrementally.

Lap by lap the coast of me erodes against the tides, breaks me down, taking some part of me away and leaving me closer to the bone, raw and exposed.

Who am I? What happened to me? I don't remember being like this as a boy. Hell, now I can't even remember being a boy.

The radio and her soft voice hoists me from the well of myself as I glance at her sing-along face as her delicate bare foot resting on the dash taps little toe prints on the slanted glass of the windshield with a certain childlike oblivion.

She doesn't see the serpents and shadows that I can't seem to elude. She seems completely unaware of my catalogue of shadows or my fallen brothers whose cries still wake me. She can't feel the guilt I wear for coming out of that mess alive and physically whole. Or if she does see them, she has some deeper faith that her love can make me whole.

She placed all her tomorrows in my pocket with her heart and her keys and some gum. I don't chew, but she loves to ask me for a stick of gum so I can give her something, which makes her feel I love her, and I do, and I don't, and I do.

We find a little road that was never lost but takes us from the traffic and the world so we stop the machine and get out.

We sit in a field, watching cows constantly chewing and looking at us with a palpable disinterest as we make our little sandwiches and drink our bottled water.

I sprawl backwards on the blanket she threw across the grass with such careful exactness. Each corner spread flat in perfect evenness, and I follow the patterns and shapes in the passing clouds that move across the sky like some ghost of a Macy's parade.

My tongue finds each morsel of flavor that hangs in corners of my mouth and I delight in each tiny discovery even more than the large bites they had escaped from. Like when I eat a bowl of ice cream, after whole spoonfuls of it gone I scrape the bottom and gather what little bits are here or there and savor them. Why do I wait for things to be almost gone before I really appreciate what I have?

She lays her head on my chest and her hand holds my body with that rare tenderness that only women truly possess. And she listens to my heart like some distant music.

I can smell her hair and feel the heat of her at each point where our bodies meet in the perfection of two jigsaw pieces found.

I want everything to stop, to lock down this moment forever so it will not fall apart into the future or the past, never to change or evolve, to lie here with her in unending stillness.

What did I know? I was so young and we had a mission. Our orders. It was our job. We were doing our duty. We didn't really think about it at the time. During the time at base camp when not out in the bush we worked the incoming and outgoing traffic, messages to airbases. We didn't realize that the orders we sent and received were death warrants. We couldn't comprehend what hell resulted from our efficiency. Highly classified high priorities passed through our comcenter in rivers of information. We routed them like happy birthday telegrams, jotted down the comings and goings and then took our cigarette breaks while F-4s tore into the sky with deadly purpose. Attack helicopters miles away left the ground bristling with armaments and laden with soldiers. And people, yes people had their bodies and their lives torn to shreds. B-52s would carpet bomb the north. What an innocent sounding word, "carpet."

Once you realize the truth of it. Once the horrible reality comes to your consciousness, once all those crows make a nest in your soul how do you ever go back? How do you ever forgive yourself? How?

She knows something's there inside me, but she doesn't mind my shadows because she somehow sees some daylight inside me that I lost track of a long time ago. She believes in my pulse even when I feel no heartbeat, even when I forget to breathe.

She knows something. She is something. Someone. I hold on. In her is something that makes me want to try.

Eventually we have to get going again so we angle our way across the map into the snow lands where once winter comes the sky stays gray until you've had enough of yourself and you have to let someone else in just for the heat and the hope.

It's a different world back east, and maybe once there I can shake the ghosts from my flesh, maybe there I can find my reflection, but for the moment I have the road, the wheel I cling to, a world seen passing in all directions through glass. The speed, the shocks, the soft seat and the radio. And every inch of the way she is with me.

After a long day of driving we finally surrender to the night in a small B&B run by an old woman whose hair has been in a bun since the Korean War, which was also the last time she creased her face with a smile. That was before someone didn't come home. Since then her life became counting pillowcases and towels and with a gray eye trying to figure out what was wrong with you. With anyone she came across who lodged in her place.

She shows us to our room. It's a postage stamp with an overhead light, a faded mirror on an old vanity that screams "Edgar Alan Poe"

The wallpaper makes promises of The Great Depression, the bed squeaks and creaks and sags under our weight. An old swayback nag ready for gluing.

The toilet paper in this joint is cruel, like some sort of Jesuit Penitent's revenge.

Even though the bed is big enough for three, we spend the night rolling towards the center of gravity so that we crowd each other. Two pressed hams in a store window, impossible to move apart in the uphill struggle. So we sleep as best we can as one giant two-headed knot of arms and legs.

I sleep but it's in an old jungle echo, with the flat thudding beat of helicopters. I can feel the wet heat crush me, and the stinging insects using me like a cheap buffet. Surrounded by teenage faces masked in fear while the crack and whizzing of gunfire rips through the foliage as it buzzes past our ears. And then the rain. That forever rain that comes down on you and in you and is everything everywhere, and doesn't give a damn about you or your life or the drama of your situation.

There's yelling and noise everywhere. I can smell the metallic bite of gunpowder. Someone is begging for his mother while someone else cries out to a god who just isn't interested.

My heart, frantic and confused. How the hell did I get back here? Why is this happening again?

I explode back to the present. I don't recognize the room. I can't put it all together. Where the hell am I? And then I see her there. Adrift in her universe. A small, warm creature who always ends up right next to me no matter how large the bed and how much room she has, only this time it's gravity that pulls us both to the center.

I drop back into the pillow and study the ceiling until fatigue takes charge again. She nuzzles up even closer without waking, making a little noise that makes me want to build a fortress around her forever. But she wakes and looks at me through the half darkness. Her soft stare reads me. Every unspoken agony, every injury, all my broken compasses are there in her glance. And she places her delicate arm across my chest, places the smallest kiss on my face and whispers "Shhhh," and it is I who is safe, and she is the castle walls. Through the night until daylight.

The morning breakfast table is a gathering of driftwood and nomads exchanging curt hellos, nods and shallow smiles in the required civility while under the critical eye of the antique egret as she serves runny eggs, hash browns and viscous coffee that tastes like canal water.

Finally the ignition puts all that behind us and we are back to it, the blacktop vein.

After a couple of hours we stop in a small gas station along a farm road that looks as if it hasn't had a customer since Bonnie and Clyde, and this lanky stick figure pumps our gas, cleans our windshield and gives us directions in a laconic full service haze of rustic indifference. I guess this young rube hasn't heard that the rest of the world has gone to self-service. Doesn't he know the planet is no longer that courteous and that it is now every man for himself?

I don't like the cold. I don't have the right clothing nor temperament for it.

The sun starts to show its age as winter makes its warnings felt through the dying air and summer rapidly fades into some nostalgic recollection.

What the hell am I doing? Why am I going in this direction? Am I being pulled or pushed. What force is at work that keeps me heading north and east?

We should've been barreling into Mexico where I could've hidden in a tan and gotten lost in a jungle of excuses and margaritas.

She wouldn't have cared, she'd have gone anywhere with me and we could've become fat *turistas* living for a while high on our greenbacks, but the car made its mind up and like an old stable horse, once pointed towards the barn there is no convincing it otherwise, we are going where we are going. Wherever that is.

Another stop, another small motel, another set of sheets.

She falls off into the dream space while my unsympathetic night mind gets caught up in the gears again. Like a song that won't leave my head, some ditty I never

liked but was on a continuous loop over and over again.
Dripping water or fingernails on a blackboard or some part
of myself that just won't leave the room.

Hour upon hour ticks by, an inventory of seconds,
each one ornately decorated with every doubt and failure of
my life, echoing like sarcastic laughter. Faces of lost
comrades. Brothers in arms who will never see their hair
turn gray or their children born while I bitch about the petty
crimes of my soul.

Where do I get the nerve to be anything but
grateful? I mean I'm alive, I've traveled, met fine people,
made good love, ate well, and seen a lot. And sure,
everyone has crap to deal with. That's life! Get over it!

She can sleep, she can always sleep, in a car, a bed,
on the side of the road, in a movie theatre, through a raging
fire, anywhere. It's a gift. A blessing from somewhere.
How does she do it?

I've spent so many hours listening to the heave and
whisper of her breathing, the soft curl of her body at rest
while I suffered the passing headlights that threw
collapsing rectangles of the window across the ceiling and
walls, or the thunderous chopping of the clock tearing away
night in a brutally slow meter.

Not just her, everyone I've ever slept with, it's
always the same. They'd drop into the well of narcosis
while I'm on trial in this darkness, and the nights would
crawl across me like sandpaper ants.

My ex wife could always fall asleep so easily. My
ex wife! About to reenlist in the marriage world. She's
found a way to put me so far behind her that she can look
ahead. She has reopened her heart for business while I still
have all my windows boarded up.

But I am here, and it is now and words, ideas,
images, memories and fear assail me. Always some thread
passing back to that stain of fear. A gnawing doubt,

unanswered questions, a life not quite attained, this monologue or dialogue of questions and accusations that open me up with surgical intrusions that leave me exposed without anesthetics. Blah, blah blah. What the hell?

I can never seem to turn away from myself, and so the hours pile up until I'm crushed under the weight of fatigue and grab a few thin hours of rest. And then at dawn there she is waking with a smile and ready to roll.

How does she do that? Doesn't she know the world is a constant carnage of everything eating everything else? A place of toxic greed and cruelty? That there's a shortage of parking spaces and an abundance of dust that carries hordes of mites and other irritants into your mouth and nose and ears?

We load up and start to roll again a large bead of water slams into the windshield. The introductory note of a liquid symphony.

The rain has two faces. It can run over everything, an anointing rush of forgiveness that removes the burden of pain and sin, or it gathers up the full concert of tears that press against the dam of human sadness until the clouds can no longer contain it all and we are caught in the rage of memories that fall upon us.

Then the sky starts to swell in a dense avalanche of brooding cumulus dread, consuming the landscape as it tumbles in from the east and we rush towards each other in a self-destructive howl of inevitability since that's the way we're headed.

Behind us a crack of silver fading light leaves a scar across the tiny horizon of the rear-view mirror and there is no turning back, so we lean into our advance with a certain gleeful fatalism, a charged sense of being alive, firing off in every atom of our bodies, a palpable electricity in the air that gives the most minute details meaning.

I can see it coming down the highway, a curtain or a wall way off in the distance, moving towards us. Another drop explodes on my windshield. An angry messenger or advance troop. Then another, a fourth, and finally the onslaught has begun, and we've got no vote in the matter.

Sheets of water pound us in some vindictive rage. Challenging us to stop or surrender, beating the world around us with an irresistible fury. The constant tattoo on the metal roof. Rivets driven into beams, the futile struggle and metronome of the wipers, oncoming headlights like fires seen through tears.

I love it, I love it all.

I can feel my passion and my defiance as my foot presses down on the gas. I can smell the wetness and the oil. To me it's a mixture of snare drums, gunfire and applause. The thunder cracks are timpani and artillery and all sorts of ordinance both real and remembered. I love it, I hate it and I love it.

Her hands white knuckle on the dash with eyes blazing insanely and through her fear a hint of a smile, that sensation of being really alive in the midst of unbridled chaos, the clarity of being when you can't really see or hear or control anything. It is ecstatic and frantic and manic.

At times she gives out a roller-coaster scream as a semi blasts by in the opposite direction throwing an even more intense wave of water into our cycloptic view, and she follows it with an almost imperceptible giggle .

I love her. This mad woman. This pixie demon so fragile and yet so defiant. I want to lash her to my side and tempt the sirens. Risk the treacherous rocks of living. Fly up to the sun until our wings melt and we fall to the earth together.

In these moments I know who she is. In this mad turbulence I see the courage she usually hides from the world come bursting to the surface, overflowing as she dances between terror and pure elation. The wipers clicking, the engine growling, thunder, lightning, splashing smashing mayhem.

If there was some way to make this moment last, to bind it to our hearts and release it when the death of routine seeks to numb us with tedium or ennui and threatens to turn us against ourselves or each other.

If we can let this dragon fly no minute would lack the thrill of being alive. No minute portion of any second would pass by unnoticed or unappreciated.

Oh god , could we? can we make it last forever?

We roll on in the madness for hours, just struggling to see ahead, forgetting all that we'd left behind. Mile after mile as it keeps coming down.

But eventually we have to find shelter before night and the storm together overwhelm us, and our Detroit time machine can no longer guarantee our safe transport.

So we are forced to return to reality. Another small roadside motel belonging to no national chain, with no familiar corporate logo burnt into our retinas, no associated jingles or slogans, just some little, old style family motel that somehow still lives in a universe of corporate giants.

We hide there for the night and in the predictable assortment of furniture and simplicity we make savage love and fall asleep under crisp sheets while clothing dries on hangers in the bathroom and the outside world keeps raining.

There is magic in the darkness once we actually surrender to it. When we go to sleep and collapse into the abyss we deconstruct and lose who we are in the disintegration of our personalities. Dropping into some primordial electric impulses we disassemble, we break up into the ethers reuniting with the limitless particles of the everything.

We lose ourselves, our names, our pasts, we stop being who we are and just are.

Fragments of chemicals and energy mixing in the great soup. Too deep for dreams or any awareness of self we fragment into our tiniest component parts and head out in all directions.

And each day starts out blank and unassigned. A chance to start over, fresh, clean, unburdened. But as we rise to the surface of consciousness we reassemble. We collect up our personal myths and histories and piece them together. We gather up all the shards of memories. Every recollection large and small gets jigsawed back into the right spots until we open our eyes and face the world as the same creature we were in the darkness of the previous night.

An opportunity lost. So we drag out all our old injuries and burdens and start lugging them around with us again.

I turn the key and the engine growls to life. Her door slams shut and I know we are ready. Oh that sensation when you just start to roll, when you go from standing still into motion. You are moving and once again things can happen.

Mornings after the rains the world is so still and wet and all the colors are richer with a certain sadness, but the fresh smell and the tender emerging light makes a promise that anything is possible, maybe even something good.

Early hours, my favorite time, when most everything and everyone has not yet joined in and you get to see the planet born once again. In the stillness you can drive alone towards the infant sun, no traffic, a quietude, undisturbed emptiness even in a man made world.

She falls back asleep almost as soon as we hit the onramp and the steady roll of the interstate gets underneath us.

I keep the radio off and softly drum my fingers on the wheel in syncopation with her breathing, the motor's groan, the tires' song, a symphony of tiny details, small intimate noises.

I steal glances at her, eyes closed, trusting me to keep her safe, keep us moving along, to make everything all right and I fill with this sense of dread. It all comes rushing back in and shatters the peace.

Why does this keep happening? Why think these thoughts?

How can I keep her world in order when mine is so out of control, when inside of me there is a war, a disaster area? Can't she see I'm under siege, torn apart with uncertainties, no idea where I'm going in life or why.

Just going.

And still she loves me. I look at her again and I fight back. I can't let her down. I can't disappoint trust like that. And she readjusts herself and I smile. Even I can't resist it. I find a small glint of light in that tiny movement of her form and I hang onto it. I use it to push away everything else and just face the road.

Slicing through the southern tip of Illinois the sky again rips open and falls to the earth. Lightning tears jagged lesions in the flat metal backdrop of clouds painted with shadows and rife with threats.

Thunder and rain beat down on us, constantly changing light as the world tries to tear itself apart. The wipers straining desperately to give us sight. The drag under the chassis each time we burst through a dip where water had gathered.

She wakes to this mad opera a bit startled, not sure where she is.

The heavens rupture and bleed a soulless fury onto us and I know we'll have to sit this one out, it's too much. So I pull onto the shoulder where gravel crunches us to a stop.

I kill the engine.

Now the liquid nails strafe our metal roof so loudly we have to yell our conversation. We undo our seatbelts and weave our arms and legs together as her warm cheek presses against mine. She hears my whispers. My small words that seep out from the very well of me and into her soul.

In the midst of all this pandemonium, this cacophonous din of percussion is a certain serenity. We simply hold each other. An eerie sense of order, a calm disrupted only when some eighteen-wheel leviathan explodes past us in defiance of the blinding rain.

I always seem to find myself, or see myself clearly when in a real crisis. When the world is actually gone mad and someone must maintain. Something clears away the debris of my ego and lets me see it all in a composed clarity. Everything slows down and I know who I am and what I'm supposed to do. I'm great during a real catastrophe. This strange reaction to catastrophe got me through the war. I somehow kept my head. Knew instinctively what to do. I was often the calming voice in the bedlam.

It is in the safety of sanity, the tedium of day-to-day where I am lost. When all the little tasks and chores are asked of me in order to live. That is where I cannot breathe, where I am the most confused, where the universe is most hostile and unsettling. In the soothing lawns of civil society is where I am the most bewildered.

But when everything is turned upside down and she needs my strength, when the demons are in the air, that's when I know who I am.

I kiss her neck and breathe her, and each sigh it produces from her, each moan, feeds me and makes me male.

The taste of her flesh, her mouth, the watery look when we glance into each other's eyes, the uneven breathing, the way the car becomes heated and steamy, the rain now underscoring each intimate border crossed until the fever takes us.

Naked in the back seat we make a slow, primitive fire that consumes us, overtakes us, pulls us from our humanity and into the savage reality of our animal natures. No part of us goes unexplored, no barriers can contain us, no rules of propriety go unbroken.

There is a cruel tenderness that we have to have and so we ride each other with a building tempo that matches the storm outside, makes it impossible for us to know where we are, and all that is real is this passion, this madness, each other.

The time passes and the sun never takes command again but the rain does ease enough to set us loose, so once again we press northeast in the steady drip and drizzle.

She goes back to her book while I listen to some country preacher static coming and going on the only reception I can get over the radio. He talks about the great flood and Jesus, and sins, and hell, and being saved, and then back to damnation, and witnessing to non-believers.

And it goes on and on, like an old man trying to scare children while a chorus of white-haired check writers supply the "live" in-studio "amens" and "halleluiahs." The perfect spooky story for such a tired light of a dying day.

And I wonder what he knows of demons and devils. The real horrors and not the phantoms of myth, but of the things let loose when men are pitted against one another. When all our genius is used to improve the fatality of our efforts. When the sons of mothers destroy the sons of mothers. When total strangers become each other's killers. What does this fire and brimstone orator know of hell? Doesn't he know it is us? We are it?

In time we have to stop and find yet another place to sleep. We need warmth and room to unlock our bodies.

The road is a string of little rooms and fresh towels. It's a big country from coast to coast, and it never lets you forget.

The headlights sweep across the little office window of The Delight Roadside Motel illuminating a rotund Lautrec moon of a face that rises from a sandwich and coffee as I wet foot up to the counter.

He smiles through the crumb hunt his tongue conducts as his eyes run over my clothing trying to determine how much he can say the rates are.

We stumble exhausted into just another room set up with that cookie cutter familiarity yet always so alien and removed. But a bed and warm shower is sometimes all you need to tell yourself that the world is still functioning with some degree of order even if it is just a lie of motel shampoo and ironed sheets.

Room 107 is an all night soap opera of marital discord that includes us in every detail through the tissue thin walls, so we keep a tally of the insults on the small bedside pads and laugh into our pillows when a particularly good score is made, but finally we fall asleep.

Yeah, sometimes I sleep.

As always the morning comes much too soon, so we bum the bed right up to checkout time and make our exit. I guess we really needed the rest. There's something about starting your day late that no matter how much you rush you can never really catch up. There's a feeling that something has been taken from you and yet you're never really sure what it is, but once you catch the flow of traffic and settle into the groove the road is always so forgiving.

We leave the Interstate for a while to get away from cruel repetition of chains. Fast food franchises, fuel stop conglomerates, and the way the highway keeps you from any reality of the place you're tearing through. Six lanes of well-kept bypass surgery.

The smaller state roads and such, let you see the houses and farms and what's left of the independent motels and gas stations. You get a chance to slow the mind and all sorts of things start to seep in through the cracks. The mind gets to imagine about the lives lived in these offbeat places. You read the local roadside ads about lawyers, Rotary Clubs, the small church announcements, the Moose Lodge, diners and coffee shops with a family name or a cute local pun.

We're both quiet for a while so I start that old x-ray of my life.

Seems I've always been chasing or avoiding or dancing around reality. There's this feeling that the taut string that holds everything together is just about to snap, that all the ropes and pulleys and mirrors projecting meaning and order will eventually come crashing down and expose me to the raw anarchy and panic of truth, that somehow I never really belonged here to begin with.

I used to imagine or dream or hope I was an orphan, or from another planet or that I'd discover that I had super powers that I could use for good and finally be loved and adored for the wonderful being who resides beneath all this noise and posturing that keeps me locked in and the world locked out.

School was hard time for me, my mind was always wandering. I couldn't understand how the other kids could sit there and listen endlessly to the drone of facts and dates and numbers that we were to jot down and memorize. The math that tied me to the rock with its no nonsense rules that were constant and rigid, the homework punishment that followed us home and wouldn't leave me alone, free to play and imagine.

I'd sit in my sixth grade class, always trying to get as far to the back of the room as possible to be as out of sight from the sniper questions that undressed me with confessions of having not done the reading. Not done the homework. That I was "unprepared" again.

I would lay low at the rear looking at the backs of the heads all lined up. I'd watch the hands shoot up with answers to the endless inquisition and wonder who they were and how they made this all work.

There were times, I recall, when I decided it was all fake, that there were no other people, just me, and that in fact I was everyone, and if I could concentrate hard enough I could slip inside any of them and have all the answers, I could have the work done, I could be prepared and not fear discovery and the public humiliation of the ensuing chastisements.

But I never could unlock that mystery and stop being myself for even a minute, no, not as a boy or a man. College on the GI Bill was easy for me. I did all the work and discovered how good I was. I guess the army changed my relationship to authority and also I was now curious about what was in those books. I had a hunger to know more things. But not so as a boy.

My old man didn't help. His short fuse and quick slap only taught me how to flinch. He didn't finish school because he had to work. He was critical and punishing when my grades were low, yet never really spent time helping me with homework. No, he was always exhausted and used up from work. Yet he had the energy to take me apart with words, and he resented that I would not surrender. That I was defiant to his will even as a very small boy.

I joined the army right out of high school at the height of the war. Yeah, even war seemed a step up from home. An escape from pain. While in my skull all those old films ran in loops of glory and courage. Of men rising to the occasion with gut and grit and bravery. No one bothered to inform us of the wailing cries of agony in a symphony of terror and uncertainty. Who knew the world was that insane? Why didn't they discuss what anti personnel weapons do to a human body? That a fire fight was all noise and madness, and that afterwards the battlefield was a garbage pail of wasted flesh and bones. No one mentioned the flies. The millions of flies who then attend the feast that you have to swat away as you try and bag and tag your comrades to be evacked back to parents who get to bury their children. You give your government your son and in exchange you get an American flag folded into a triangular shape.

I'm sorry, but I somehow missed where the glory was.

Yeah, I enlisted to get away from my family in search of myself and some inner peace. Ha!

By mid afternoon we are getting hungry again and even though I hate to stop, ever, we pull into a little place that has a neon sign claiming "Home Cooking," which in my case feels more like a threat than a promise.

But she has more trust than I do and the parking spot is waiting for us right out front, so who can resist fate?

The place has a folksy quality that feels real, not like some LA joint with faux old tin Coca Cola signs and sepia photographs reprinted to look like they were picked up in secondhand shops. No, this is the real dog. This small town is all secondhand. An honestly lived in, used, chunk of authentic America.

When I was a kid in New York I used to wonder how people could live anywhere but New York, I thought it was the center of the universe. I was sure that everyone everywhere was hoping, waiting for the day, struggling to move to New York so they wouldn't be missing anything since nothing else really happened anywhere else. But after years of not living there I came to realize that people live full lives without even really thinking of the city

To many folks it's just a backdrop to a movie, or a place to criticize through stereotype ideas and broad stroke images, but they don't envy or desire to live there, they are where they are, where they know, and they're not leaving.

Some folks do have the New York City dream, so they stream in from all over the world and love it. Others, come, feel the press and decide they were better off in Akron or Ames or Sedona, and they're gone.

The waitress is a middle-years woman who looks like she had some high school beauty at one time.

What is it about women who hit their 40s and cut their hair short and puff it up into some sort of unnatural helmet that wouldn't move in a tornado?

We order the special, which places before us enough food for us to invite guests over or cater a small wedding.

Alone the two of us sit there, and across the table I watch her eat. She is all light and fireflies. Everything excites her and nourishes her. Her eyes blaze. I watch every bite she takes, the way she closes her mouth and delicately chews, and then resumes her happy observations of the life around her. She's almost always the prettiest woman wherever we go. Not in some loud announcement, but in a quiet, steady beauty that runs inside and out. I mean, once you notice her it's really unmistakable. This woman is alive.

I marvel at her, envy her, pity her, love her, I'm afraid of her. Afraid that at some point she'll look at me and see all the broken pieces and decide not to tinker any longer on this repair job of a man.

But for the moment all is well until some local with a 23 inch neck and a size two hat notices our California plates and decides we had to be ridiculed for his droning life. The plates weren't even ours, they came with the car.

He starts his invective loud enough that we can hear his sarcasm from tables away, and his semi-evolved buddy laughs through mashed potatoes and corn. Saying something about California, queers and flakes.

Her eyes lock on mine begging me to be deaf. She knows my prideful foolishness. She wants to eat and move on.

Funny how a license plate, a mere bureaucratic registration of where you park your car can be a red cape, a tribal banner that evokes some xenophobic ire, a challenge of some sort.

The waitress' apologies flow with the coffee refills but the Cro-Magnon keeps firing arrows into our campsite, I chew my food and bit my tongue because my girl wants me to.

All my life there have always been these guys. Something missing in their lives, or their genetics that always made them feel that someone else was responsible for their misery and someone had to pay.

My father boxed professionally for a while when he was young, and so I grew up a boxer's son, and while coming up I had to go around in circles with neighborhood lugs who took my jabs and crosses and were unable to answer back as they swung at where I used to be.

For a long time I had to take on guys I didn't even know just because they heard I was good and had to test me in order to find their spot in the ranking so they could feel like somebody.

They felt like somebody, somebody with a bloody nose or a fat lip, or an eye that swelled shut in a rainbow of colors.

The flesh can be rather articulate.

After a while you get a solid enough name and the contestants stop coming, but that was a few lifetimes ago and in another part of the planet, and to these sub-mongoloids I'm just another California cookie.

Ignoring a barking dog can do one of two things, tire the dog out so he stops, or it makes him bolder so he'd push closer to test his intimidation.

Tweedledee must've hit his limit because he lumbers over to our table in the big belly walk that always requires an adjustment of the belt buckle. He looms over our table like Mighty Joe Young in a plaid shirt, and leans down on his Volkswagen sized fists and pushes his face in closer to mine and says something about kicking my ass. I smile and tell him he'd better bring a lunch because it's gonna take him all day.

He swings at me with a clumsy right which I avoid by falling backwards in my chair and rolling to a standing position and then I throw a quick stabbing jab at his face which opens a small cut on the bridge of his nose. It has always served me in these situations to have bony knuckles.

But the meat wagon keeps at me so I pop him twice more with the left and then catch him under his left cheek hard with an overhand right, but he's still coming. I hate when that happens.

I can't tell if there is screaming or country music or sirens in the background because all I can hear is my breathing and his footsteps as his boots drag his fat ass closer all the time.

I dance and punch and slip and move and he takes everything I can throw at him, his eyes a rage of fury and frustration as we bang into tables creating a mess, but I keep moving just out of reach and I'm cutting his mug with each stinging blow when he catches me with a hook that comes from some other county and I find myself on the floor a few feet away from where I was standing, and I'm pretty sure a bus must've crashed through the side of the diner and landed on my face.

There a certain calm comes over me and my head clears, a detachment of sorts as I see this wounded animal storming towards me, I can tell my lip was bleeding and swollen but I don't really feel anything.

He comes racing in to grab me with his bear intentions but as soon as his face gets low enough I kick it with both feet like a spring released and there is a definite crunching noise of some sort which follows him back all the way to the table he crushes as his beanstalk collapses.

I get to my feet and wait for his buddy to pick up the slack but his face has nothing on it but "get me outta here."

The waitress runs to me with a towel full of ice and an embarrassed song of "I'm so sorry" and refuses my money so we leave.

Yeah, it's just like home cooking after all.

She drives. My head tilted back with icepack pressing against a golf ball lip and a nose that's trying to drain my head of all the blood in it.

I feel everything now, every capillary in my head, my face, every pebble we drive over, every inch of America that we pass over. Oh how I long for the sterile safety of the Interstate.

I take that punch again a dozen times through the night, each time waking to her easy inhale exhale while she touches me with as many parts of her body as she can. Even in her sleep she's making sure I'm real, making sure I'm there.

The bleeding finally stops but I know it will be a day or two before I can have food without pain, drink without a straw.

The sun breaks through small openings in the clouds leaving a dappled design on everything the morning touches.

Driving again my tongue plays with the swelling and ground beef wound inside my mouth. My body is still sore and even my knuckles are bruised and cut as they swing left and right atop the steering wheel. I can still smell a little blood in my nose and occasionally a drop runs down my throat.

She looks at me quizzically because she notices I'm smiling. And then I start to laugh. She wants to know what's so funny when I'm obviously in such pain. When I catch my breath I tell her the I just imagined what the other guy's day must be like since I know I busted his nose and maybe even his jaw.

She shakes her head and with a wry smile quietly mumbles, "Men."

A glance in the rearview mirror and I catch a glimpse of myself, of the endless struggle of my life, a biography of scars, each mark no matter how small, a chapter, and through all the rough terrain of who I am she sees something beautiful, something worth saving, or hanging onto, and I keep trying to trust her insights.

Sometimes you find who you are in someone else. They're the only mirrors to believe in. You measure yourself by the quality of those who love you. So maybe I'm all right. Maybe.

I push the crate hard into the late afternoon's fading light, stopping only for gas, oil, and sandwiches, not much conversation, but little is needed, her being there was saying enough to sustain me.

I don't want to stop as night is taking over and the landscape disappearing. Not much to see on the interstate in southern Indiana anyway so I hook onto a pace car and make pretty good time on the wrong side of the law, but by one a.m. I am starting to collapse in on myself and so I pull into a rest area, lock all the doors and fall into the pocket of darkness.

I'm somewhere deep in the jungle. I hear the ripping sound of rounds tearing through the dense foliage. There's yelling and that stinging crack of small arms fire. Someone is howling for the medic while off a mere few meters ahead I hear the same pleas in a language so foreign to me and yet something I hear every day. The pump of adrenalin, the way your eyes and ears grow keen. All senses on full. How insane is this?

The bellowing engine startups of semis with the elephantine exhales of their airbrakes wrenches me from sleep with a primitive urgency. Takes me a few minutes to reorient myself, remember where I am, who I am, and she merely shifts positions.

Must've rained a little, all the windows are dotted with water and everything has that tender wet light.

I kick the horses and we are going again.

She finally wakes up, smiling, always smiling as if she knows something about the day that makes all the rodents and earthworms in my head seem so foolish. And then a morning kiss that puts the previous night behind me. I'm in America.

She loves the rain, the way it brings the sky down to us, the way it makes cars whisper as they pass, the way it reveals the deep glaze of the true colors of everything that are normally hidden under the ash of life. How the rain forces people to quickstep behind collars and under umbrellas and newspapers, how they crowd doorways like birds, and keep looking upwards as if some hint would be coming forth, the tiptoed run trying to avoid the deep spots. She loves all of it.

She turns on the radio and finds some piano blues that seems to know exactly what we both are feeling even though we are feeling such different things.

Indiana dissolves into Ohio in secret, if there were no signs you'd never know, it just changes hands without a hint, no wink of the eye, no nod, nothing, it just starts being Ohio.

By traveling so low in these states we hit mostly farmland and avoid the industrial muscle of the northern counties, the part where the clouds rise from the earth instead of dropping from the sky. Where smokestacks never sleep and work whistles bring rugged hands online and the nation's skeleton is built. No, down here it's farms and small towns.

The days all run together and I'm not even sure how long we've been on the road. The deserts of the southwest seem so remote and unbelievable, something imagined or heard of but nothing possible. This part of the world has so many trees and shrubs and growth even this late in the season.

We are getting closer to somewhere, or further away.

Finally Pennsylvania lets us in and we now have to work our way across the Keystone State with its mountains and fields, so many farms.

Something has erupted inside of her as if she suddenly can sense something. Finally we are really somewhere else that we've actually covered some ground and we are getting somewhere. It's "eastern." No more of that feeling of the west. Something different is in the air itself. In the landscape. She senses it. But then the car starts to make a noise I don't like, some squealing whine from hell that wakes us both from the rapturous reverie that fills you whenever you somehow are able to escape the awareness of how many forces in the universe are working against you.

All the disease ridden insects that want your blood, all the savage animals that want your flesh, plants that could eat away the top layers of f skin with their toxic saps, all the microbes and bacterium looking for a human host to feed off of and eventually destroy your health.

And all accidental bumps and bruises and cuts that can infect or maim you, the major body slams that can break and ruin you, the intentional assaults from the knuckles of some pinhead with a hair up his ass.

The unending onslaught of insults, humiliations, rejections that aim to cripple your spirit, shrink your soul, shatter your dreams.

And of course all the little bulbs, circuits, connectors, valves, springs, switches and microchips that fry, snap, peel, pop, rust and go to pieces just when you need them most.

We were lost in that delightful ignorance, but now, right now, the car is dragging us back to the world as it is. Imperfect and full of hassles.

We get off onto the shoulder and come to a stop, exchange looks of "who needs this?"

I get out of the car.

I leave the motor running so I cam see if I can find the source of this banshee wail. I look down on the mystery of wires and cables coming and going from here and there on this hulking metal array of nuts and rivets and blocks and pans all basted in a viscous coat of grease and burnt carbon.

I have her step on the accelerator and the beast cries out in a lament of agony and I, in my profound state of semi-ignorance deduce that it is the fan belt which is heroically trying to function while shredding under the stress of this long journey.

I don't have any tools, and even if I had them, I'm not a mechanic, I can change a tire or the oil, or some other minor repair, but I don't know what to loosen or how to put it back in order to replace a fan belt even if I have one to replace the worn one with.

I walk up the road a mile while she waits with the car. Luckily I find a roadside phone and soon I'm walking back hoping the auto club is prompt and efficient because I hate waiting.

I'm always the one waiting, I'm prompt, I'm pathologically prompt, so I'm always the one waiting no matter whom I'm meeting with, where or when.

Sometimes I've intentionally held myself back, slowed down, trying to be late just so I can experience walking up and seeing whomever it was I was going to meet standing or sitting there waiting for me. But no, even then I'd always end up looking at my watch and looking around, waiting. It's my fate.

So I hate just sitting there losing the time we had been so effectively making, but I get back to the car and we sit there, and wait, and wait some more.

After a while we can see the tow truck coming down the road from out of the west and we exhale.

We stand by in that foolish helplessness while a skeleton in filthy overalls wrestles the bolts loose and changes the fan belt.

I watch his honest hands working the joints and wrenches with familiarity.

I wonder if he ever got those nails clean, if he touches his wife or his woman with those abused mitts. I wonder about his dreams and what he was like as a boy.

He gets us straight and I give him some cash to buy some beers and I carry him for miles until my mind drops him off in a dull sadness. I wonder also why I do that. Why I see each life as a biography.

How does a man end up that way? What choices did he make along the way? What fate was thrust upon him to make him labor endlessly in the tar of life, to welter in the struggle that only grows as his body tires with time?

There's no conversation in the car, there's nothing for either of us to say, some part of each of us seems to know that we are fortunate, that our fates are somehow still unwritten, that we are still making choices and that all the doors still seem to be open and it was yet up to us to walk through whichever ones we choose.

We find a small motel off the main highway. A tucked away row of paint starved bungalows. Quiet and tired we drop off quickly, her head on my chest, her leg over my leg until the next day breaks in and we were at it again.

This routine of rising and running and stopping and going has become everything we know, there is only the road, everything we had been and done before we'd started was no longer ours, was no longer us. We'd become this motion. We are this thing that moves ever eastward with no explanation. Without a plan or even a discussion. Just pushing on. Stopping for the necessities of food, fuel and rest and that's it.

Soon western Pennsylvania becomes central Pennsylvania becomes eastern Pennsylvania and New Jersey is waiting dead ahead.

California is now a faded photograph that someone once showed me in a distant dream of gentle weather, the sprawl of humanity, the unending stretch of coastline.

The palm trees, some long and tall and bending high into the sky, sculpted by the offshore winds into graceful arching curves, some thick with spiny barks and robust crowns of dark green fronds all year long. And somewhere on that far rim of this continent where the Pacific puts a stop to all the roads heading west, my ex gets a cold, glittering stone for her finger, and our shared past gets buried beneath it.

But here and now it's the solid gray skies of the northeast, brilliantly painted leaves falling and leaving naked each tree's architecture. The bite of night air awaiting the imminent attack of winter that will come crashing down from Canada and sit there oppressively until Spring.

Why, why did I leave that ease? Why am I here? Why have I brought her to this civilized wilderness? What am I really escaping from? What am I running towards?

We break into lower New Jersey late in the day and follow the interstate north through the low flatlands with the seam of industry that is the New Jersey Turnpike.

This working man's state, a constant caravan of semis and fuel and chemical trucks, the elephant stampede of 18 wheelers rampaging towards New York or south towards D.C. with Benzedrine cowboys jittering at the wheel with their CB poetry banter. The surge of cars running north and south up and down the northeast corridor between Washington and Boston and all points in between. This is reality, this is how things get done, the veins of commerce that fuel everything, the business of living.

Soon there it is, off to our right, the first signs of the distinctive New York skyline like diamonds and precious stones set in concrete and glass and steel. Bauhaus boxes, art deco hypodermic needles that pierce deep into the dark sky, gargoyles and angels hidden in the shattered mirror mosaics and geometry that see itself reflected in the Hudson River.

She stares childlike at Oz, I can almost feel the pounding of her heart's excitement as she tries to take in this looming behemoth. If you grow up here you can't imagine what the place looks like to new eyes. You always had this as your world. But to her.

The world seem to stand in the shadow of this heaving city of millions, lashed together with bridges and tunnels, the night traffic's head and tail lights coursing through its streets like red and white corpuscles.

There is a space in the sky where two giants once stood, a scar of something missing.

Memories rise in me like revenants, familiar wraiths who peel away the veneer of maturity and composure, leave me naked as a child. All the old injuries and insults, the broken hearts, the youthful passions, the dreams of all the could-bes and endless possibilities that stretched out ahead like strings of promises lit by kisses, the songs and music and teenage summers.

We head north to the George Washington Bridge over the Hudson and into the center of Manhattan, take the Westside south to downtown.

So much had changed, the Westside Highway is gone, new buildings and wide roads, more light and less rubble as we continue south and finally find a dark street in Tribeca where we can turn off the engine and sleep.

Tucked in a backseat huddle we fall into the dark sleep while the city stays up.

New York wakes with a snarl, a growling thunder of trucks, the buzzing swarm of yellow cabs, wave upon wave of faces moving in all directions, tucked deeply into raised collars, hats, scarves, and long coats in city strides, it's a city that walks and rolls and rumbles along.

We get out into the bite of air that promises even colder days and start stepping. She tucks herself under my arm for heat.

I can see the flames in her eyes as she dines on the parade of humanity teeming through the architecture as we head up the sidewalk north and left.

The small shops along Canal Street bust open onto the sidewalk in a frenzy of Chinese, Arabs, Puerto Ricans, Jews, Armenians, Africans and all possible nationalities, arranging their tables and racks with watches and caps, pocket books and gloves, shoes, shirts, sweaters, umbrellas, trinkets and souvenirs in a clamor of Babel, the daily rebirth of commerce, the start of just another day in Manhattan.

Weary expressions, determined, lost in thought, clinging to paper cups of takeout coffee, smoking cigarettes.

Ashen, lipless Wasp bankers and brokers in dark suit-seriousness, clutching New York Times and Wall Street Journal security blankets.

Subways coughing up samples from every gene pool this earth offers.

Snap shot tourists in their mismatch stumble, bundled in souvenir clothing, get an early start at the sights as they conspicuously puzzle at maps and subway schedules.

How could I have brought this soft flicker of light into this madhouse of clamor and chaos? And yet her face is alit with awe and appetite for all of it.

In a small diner on 6th and Grand we stop for breakfast, the woman at the register takes orders to go with a strong Russian voice and a rushed courtesy. An old Irish waiter writes down our order and disappears into the noise of "dees" and "dohs."

This city belongs to no one, it belongs to everyone, the Pakistani cab drivers, the French shopkeeper, the German baker, the sons and daughters and grandchildren of Italian and Polish masons and house painters, Yeshiva students, Vietnamese and Korean produce shop owners, Haitian housekeepers, Greek computer programmers, dark skinned Caribbean women pushing white babies in strollers, Japanese, Dutch, Australians, Polynesians, every nationality, every race, this city belongs to the world.

I'd lived in the LA-boulevard, palm-tree-freeway-desert for a long time cradled in a pocket of surrounding mountains and hills, kissed by the beach air of Venice, thinking I was freezing when the temps dropped below 60 degrees.

She was born there, raised in the easy pace and forgiving weather and even after many years I always felt I had just arrived there.

The slow, laconic manana reality, the long low horizon that swallows the sun, the lazy sleepwalk along the clean sidewalks, I got used to that, even liked it, this was who I'd become, so why did I leave it to come back here, and what about her? What is here for her?

I will forever be from where I'm from, New York City. It is in my DNA, still written into my dialogue and my gestures, my glance, the way I walk or toss a smirk, no amount of Frappuccino's in the sunshine calm could ever wash away the graffiti of my soul or sedate the subway growl and street corner prowl that is forever roaming around beneath my flesh.

New York is the Rome of our day, only the emperor is in the architecture and the hustle, the noise and the rumble, solid like the bedrock it's built on, busy with the endless footsteps and traffic in the taxicab air.

New York is the "dio padre" of all cities, the very soup of humanity, it is the last human mountain. It's like living on the pounding vein, the center of the modern world.

It's not better than other places, it's just not like any other place, not like other cities that look so similar to each other with their franchise facades, and auto row scars, not the cloned suburbs of everywhere and anywhere. No, you never can mistake New York for any other place.

It is a restless gargantuan that not only consumes, but gives, creates, generates and inspires, no one industry can dominate its soul or define its stance. No one can own it or control it or even manage it, it is a living thing that both attracts and repels, it is a concrete fire, a circus of characters painted on a breathing canvas, an unforgettably elegant savage who can seduce you or break your heart.

I am glad I grew up here, half my life, survived the worst of it and the best of it, but I'm from Brooklyn, the blue collar muscle of the city, the dark eyed strut, etched with ethnic streets and tribal pride, workers' hands, wise guy angles and an attitude as unique as a fingerprint, separated by the most beautiful bridge on earth which pumps its blood back and forth adding to the bite of the town, the bearing, the humor.

Everyone's immigrant grandmother's cooking painting the air with foreign aromas and exotic accents, the pinching of cheeks and sloppy kisses and "you have to eat something… Eat something!"

Sandlot baseball, and stickball and schoolyard sneaker summers, dead car battery winters, and springtime hope after the snow is gone and the rains have stopped.

The United Nations roll call when the teacher took attendance in the mosaic of our neighborhood school.

I couldn't live here anymore. For me it is a series of chapters already read, it's the first floor of my life and I'm already on the observation deck, so I love it like an old song, or photographs that remind me of someone I used to be, but once spent, a coin must change hands.

And yet here I am, once again amongst the concrete and bricks that knew my youngest face, the giant that cradled me and watched me run the schoolyard years of handball and dodge ball, the rugged years of growing pains and wondering, the place of my yearning heart, my starving innocence. What has pulled me back to the place of my original escape?

And here I stand, with her, those eyes that smile, and she loves me with a dangerous surrender that makes me want to do great things and be someone I only hoped I could be.

I hold her face as she stares so deeply inside me that I am warm and strong and I kiss her.

And I know we will do no driving today. And in my heart I calmly wish my ex-wife the best of luck as I kiss this woman in my arms knowing she is where I live.

END

About the Author

Roy Eisenstein is a writer and director (Directors Guild of America). Originally from Brooklyn, New York, he served in the US Army from 1967 to 1970. He was in the 1st Signal Brigade, Strategic Communications, from 1968 to 1969.

Roy currently runs EyeZenMedia Productions (Eyezenmedia.Weebly.Com) out of Venice, California. You can view his short films, spoken-word pieces, and songs he wrote the lyrics for at https://www.youtube.com/EyezenMediaProds.

52252906R10038

Made in the USA
Columbia, SC
01 March 2019